1

# A

# SIGHT TO REMEMBER

## By

## Mary Grace Patterson

Dedicated to:

Joshua, our special little angel,
my friends, Nancy, Donna, Sherry,
mom, and my family

Some illustrations by:

Robert H. Patterson
P. Drew,
Rose E. Grier Evans -Writer, Illustrator, Child Advocate

Special thanks to:

Paul Holmes, Shirley George, Payton Land,
Arlene Kincaid, Nora Paulus & Author Friend, Lisa Ashley

# The Poem That Started It All

## A Sight to Remember

I was looking out of my window on Christmas Eve night.
Low and behold, I saw such a strange unusual sight!

I saw Santa in his sleigh, but no reindeer were in sight.
Instead it was pulled by flamingos who were in full flight.

Each was in harness with jingle bells attached.
They wore long red stockings and fine Christmas caps.

I saw them stop at each house on all of the streets.
They waited there patiently, as Santa delivered his treats.

When he came to our house, I pretended to be asleep.
I heard him leave, and into the sleigh he leaped.

I heard Santa shout, calling out each birds name.
The Flamingos started to move and were soon flying again.

Santa called out as they flew way out of sight,
"Merry Christmas everyone on this special night."

Mary Grace Patterson

The frigid north wind blew harder than it had in years. Large snowflakes fell like an invading army in North Pole City. Crystal designs adorned the windows of homes and workshops. Cold, powdery snow drifted against the buildings.

Inside one of the large workshops a fireplace crackled with amber flames. The scent of burning wood mingled with the aroma of a huge Christmas tree standing in the corner.

Candy canes, sugarplums, shiny stars, and pretty ornaments hung from the branches. Multicolored lights added to the tree's beauty. Santa's elves happily sang Christmas songs as they made various toys.

The door opened and Santa entered amidst a blast of cold arctic air and swirling snowflakes. "Br-r-r-r, it's cold out there," Santa exclaimed. "I haven't seen weather like this in over one hundred years."

"Yeah, you're right, it's a miserable storm," replied Jack, Santa's assistant. So far the toy making is on schedule but if the storm doesn't abate, we might not get enough supplies to complete the orders."

8

"How's Jamsey coming along with his new invention?  Every year the requests get more complicated because children ask for all the new unusual toys."

"Jamsey's invisible dragon is almost perfected.  It'll be a number one taker."

"Great!  I know the kids will love it.  He's is the best inventor in North Pole City."

The weeks went by quickly as the reindeer practiced runs, jumps, and flying so they'd be in good condition for the biggest night of the year.  An assortment of icy shapes formed on their antlers and their noses were covered with frost.  As the frigid wind continued, the reindeer struggled to keep their balance.

Robert, chief elf in charge of reindeer transportation, had a difficult time keeping the reindeer barn warm.  Three days before Christmas some of team began coughing.  Others had runny noses and appeared lethargic.  Comet, Blitzen, and Dancer developed fevers.

Soon all the reindeer had bright green noses, which indicated a severe virus.

Robert tried various cures but nothing worked. Finally, he conferred with Dr. Crystal who had been with Santa more than two hundred years. "I've never seen anything like this," Robert sighed.

Neither have I," Dr. Crystal replied. "Let's check my special book of ancient remedies. Perhaps I can find one that will help them." She looked at pages and pages of therapies. "I found it, this will surely work," Dr. Crystal cried. "Help me make this potion, Robert."

Quickly, they made the special medicine and gave it to each reindeer. The mixture made the illness worse. Their noses turned a brighter shade of green.

"Oh, dear, if this medicine didn't work, I don't know of anything else," the doctor said sadly. "We've got to tell Santa."

Dr. Crystal and Robert hurried to Santa's house. They explained the awful situation. Santa pulled on his coat and ran to the barn. Carefully, he checked each reindeer. "Oh me, oh my, what are we going to do? Have you tried everything you know, doctor?"

"Yes, Robert and I tried everything, even an ancient remedy that usually works in cases like this. The illness will have to run its course.

The reindeer are too sick to make the trip this year." Santa's face paled as reality set in.

"We must inform everyone that there will be no Christmas this year," Robert said quietly.

"We can't let that happen, Robert. We need to think of something so that Christmas can be saved," Santa shouted.

News of the reindeer's illness spread quickly through the small town. All toy making came to a halt.

"We can't cancel Christmas. There has to be a way to get my sleigh in the air," Santa cried. Robert suggested that they send fliers to everyone in the town for ideas. Santa agreed. He printed the papers and Robert and his helpers delivered them to all the homes in the small city.

All through the night Santa waited hoping someone would come up with a miracle solution to save Christmas. No one called. A tired, despondent Santa fell asleep.

Meanwhile, the warmth from the fireplace in Robert's house made him sleepy as he rested on his couch. He was almost asleep when he jumped up, falling over his boots.

"Hey, I forgot about my special thinking cap," he yelled. He ran to his closet and searched for the right box. It was on the bottom of the stack. Robert put the orange and blue cap on his head and sat in his chair.

Within seconds, Benny's name popped into his brain. Running as fast as he could, Robert burst into Santa's house without knocking.

Breathlessly, Robert cried," Santa, how about Benny?"
"Benny who?"

"Remember, Benny used to live here many years ago.
He retired and moved to Punta Gorda, Florida. He was so smart. If anyone can solve our problem, he can."


"Yes, yes, I remember him. Good idea! I'll call him right now."


Santa got Benny's phone number from the operator. Nervously he dialed the number. An answering machine came on, "Hi, this is Benny in sunny Florida. Please leave a message. I'll call you back as soon as possible."

"Hey, Benny, this is Santa. I have a desperate situation and need your help. We don't have much time. All the reindeer are sick and can't pull the sleigh. Please call as soon as you can. Thanks."

Benny was by the lake sipping an orange shake. Warm breezes blew through the tall green saw grass. "What a beautiful day," he exclaimed to his flamingo friend, Fargo, whom he met soon after he bought his house in southwest Florida. "This is southern living at its best."

Fargo and his flock stood nearby enjoying the sunshine.

Silver ripples moved across the water like soft musical notes. There was a great splash as something swam quickly toward them with its tail moving from side to side. The flamingos scattered when Ricky Alligator swam to shore.

"Hi Benny, what's up?" asked Ricky.

"Do you want to go for a ride? The water's great."

"No, thanks, I'm working on my tan."

Just then, Lizzy Squirrel scampered toward Ricky. "Take me. I want to go." Lizzy hopped on Ricky's back.

Happy to have a passenger, Ricky swam to deeper water.

Two hours later Benny and Fargo went home.
"Hey, how about some lunch?  I'm starving," said Benny.
"Sounds good to me.  I'm hungry too," Fargo agreed.
"Let's have some veggie pizza that was left over from last nights' supper."

On his way to the kitchen, Benny noticed the answering machine button blinking.  There was one message.  Benny returned Santa's call immediately.  After Santa explained his situation, Benny asked, "How did the reindeer get sick?  Did Dr. Crystal try the mustard green therapy?  How about the carrot cough syrup?"

"We don't know the cause. Yes, we tried all the medicines and nothing worked. They are too ill to pull my sleigh. Do you have any ideas for replacements?"

"Gee, Santa, I don't know right at this minute. Let me think about it and I'll call you back."

"Okay, thanks, but think fast, please. There's only one more day until Christmas Eve. I cannot disappoint all the children. They would never believe in me again if I failed to bring their presents."

Benny told Fargo about Santa's dreadful dilemma. They discussed various ideas but none were feasible.

Finally, Benny said he needed to go outside for some fresh air. His friend joined him. Birds flew in and out of the feeder. A beautiful bluebird flew away after his lunch, to a large oak tree and disappeared.

"Doesn't the bluebird fly gracefully?" asked Benny.

Before Fargo could answer, Benny shouted, "Hey, that's it! Flying birds. That's the answer."

"What? What about flying birds?"

"Fargo, do you think it's possible you and your flamingo friends can pull Santa's sleigh? Maybe that's how we can help to save Christmas."

"What a great idea," exclaimed Fargo. "I'll ask them, be right back."

Fargo's friends agreed to help. He told Benny the good news. Santa was ecstatic to receive Benny's phone call but he worried that the flamingos couldn't fly all night delivering presents and tolerate the cold weather.

Benny assured Santa that the flamingos were used to traveling and would be able to adjust to the weather conditions.

"I'll call the airlines and we'll get the next flight going north," Benny said. "The flamingos will get a good rest on the plane so they'll be ready for the big night."

"Super, thank you so much, Benny! See you soon," Santa responded excitedly.

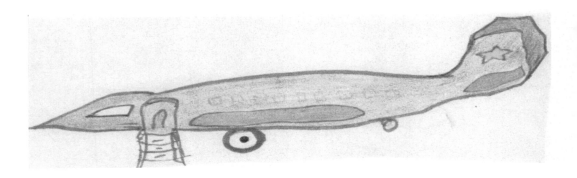

Since the group didn't have any heavy clothing, they took things that they could layer to keep them warm. Ten of the strongest flamingos boarded the plane with Benny and Fargo.

The plane landed in Alaska in the morning. Elves driving dogsleds waited to take the group to North Pole City.

The flamingos huddled under warm, battery operated blankets arriving at North Pole City at noontime. Elves cheered while the group was quickly taken to Santa's home where Mrs. Claus had cooked a special lunch.

After everyone rested a short time, then they went to the harness room. Jack, Robert, and Benny remade the jingle harnesses to fit every flamingo. They installed special heaters to keep the birds warm. Each flamingo wore insulated red stockings to cover their long legs and a red hat trimmed with white fur.

The elves packed the sleigh with presents as Fargo stood at the head of the flock. Santa settled into his special seat while Jack took many photos of the unbelievable sight. Santa laughed, "This is Christmas history! Okay, flamingos, are you ready?"

"Yes, Santa, we're ready."

"Up, up and away," shouted Santa. "Go Fargo, on Singer, Winger, Luke, Duke. On Ted, Ed, Terry, Jerry, Ike, and Spike. Bells jingled as the sleigh lifted easily into the evening sky.

The night went by quickly without any problems. They were almost finished when some flamingos slipped on an icy roof. Fargo lunged to keep the sleigh from sliding off the roof. He injured one of his wings and cried out in pain. When Santa examined him, he found it was a bad sprain. He didn't think Fargo could continue to fly.

"Don't worry, Santa," Fargo groaned. "I'll make it. The others will pull more of the weight."

At last all the presents were delivered. A tired Santa and his flock headed back to North Pole City. They arrived safely at the reindeer barn. The flamingos were relieved of their harnesses. Jack and Robert attended to Fargo's injured wing. It would heal in a few days.

Mrs. Claus hugged Santa and thanked all the flamingos. She prepared a huge Christmas breakfast. During the meal the flamingos received special gifts from Mr. and Mrs. Claus.

"I want to thank all of you for helping to save Christmas," a teary-eyed Santa said. "I am so grateful. Children are happy this morning and so am I!"

"You can be very proud of yourselves! Benny, I'd like to present you with this special present, thanking you for the greatest idea you ever had!"

"Thank you, Santa. I'm very pleased that I could help but Fargo and his friends are the real heroes."

"They certainly are," smiled Santa. "Fargo, please come forward."

As Fargo walked to the center of the room, everyone applauded and cheered. His face turned a deeper shade of pink as Santa placed a special gold medal, hanging from a blue velvet ribbon, around his slender neck.

Laughter filled the room. Good friends wished each other Merry Christmas. Memories of this unusual, happy holiday would remain with them forever.

# MERRY CHRISTMAS TO EVERYONE! MAY THE SPIRIT OF CHRISTMAS FILL YOUR HEARTS ALL YEAR LONG!

# Information about Flamingos

There are six species of Flamingos.

They are found in South America, the Caribbean, Africa, the Middle East, Europe and in parts of the United States.

The word "Flamingo" comes from the Spanish and Latin word, "Flamenco." It means fire, which refers to the bright colors of the bird's plumage.

Flamingos hold their bills upside down when they eat, so they can filter their food.

Flamingos lay only one egg a year. Their chicks and born gray and white and are that color the first three to four years of their life.

The pink or orangish color is caused by carotenoid pigments in their food, such as plankton, algae, and crustaceans. Continuous use of special foods will help them keep their color, pink or orange pink.

Most Flamingos live and travel in flocks.

# Poem: A Flamingo Christmas

Fargo Flamingo is as happy as can be,
for he and his flock made Christmas Eve history.

When Santa's reindeer became sick with the flu,
Fargo and Benny knew just what to do.

They all took a plane to Alaska's frontier,
and faced the frozen Arctic with no thoughts of fear.

Soon all arrived at Santa's secret place.
New heated harnesses were made with no time to waste.

Each flamingo wore long red stockings to cover slim legs.
A red Christmas cap was tied around each face.

All stood in line, reins attached to the sleigh,
Santa jumped in, yelled, up, up and away.

Off they flew across the ebony sky,
flapping strong wings, as the pale moon rose on high.

The toys were almost all gone,
when something went terribly wrong.

Some flamingos slipped on an icy roof. Santa's sleigh
began to sway. Fargo's quick thinking saved the day.

With a mighty lunge, he righted the sleigh,
but injured his wing. It hurt right away.

A bad sprain was detected when his wing was checked.
All thought the rest of the trip might be affected.

Fargo assured them he could continue to fly.

He grimaced with pain as the rest of the night went by.

As the sun began to rise in the early cold morn,
Santa and his tired team arrived home, fatigued and worn.

All were greeted with cheers and joyous shouts,
as the residents of North Pole City gathered about.

After the jingle harnesses were taken away,
they went to Santa' s for a special breakfast on Christmas day.

Gifts were given to all who were there.
Tired, happy, flamingos relaxed on couches and chairs.

Santa hung a bright gold medal around Fargo's slim neck.
The flamingos face turned the deepest shade of pink seen yet.

Santa still chuckles every now and then,
as he fondly remembers Fargo and his flamingo friends.

History was made on that event filled Christmas eve,
when Fargo and friends delivered presents with precision and
speed.

The spirit Of Christmas remains in all hearts.
It's felt the world over and never departs!

# Biography:  Mary Grace Patterson

I was born and raised in St. Johnsbury,
a small town in the Northeast Kingdom of Vermont.

I grew up in a home filled with music, family
gatherings, and traditions.

My northern heritage has had a deep impact on
my life, stories, and poetry.

We moved south many years ago, and reside in the
quiet countryside of Southwest Florida beside a small
lake.

My husband, Richard, and I have eight children,
his, mine, and ours.  We have been truly blessed!

I am a retired nurse and a member of the
"Peace River Writers" in Punta Gorda, Florida.

I'm also a published poet and writer.  My hobbies are
fishing, camping, boating, reading, writing, music, and
special times with my husband and family.

Florida has many tropical birds.  I was inspired
to write this Christmas tale by the beautiful flamingos
who reside here. This story is the first in a series I plan to write.

I hope that all will enjoy this epic tale of friendship, strength,
courage, and endurance.  May the spirit of the yuletide season
always remain with you.

Made in the USA
Columbia, SC
23 June 2023

18834018R00015